SPY SOCIETY

the CASE of the MUSICAL MISHAP

Veronica Mang

VIKING

VIKING
An imprint of Penguin Random House LLC, New York

First published in the United States of America by Viking,
an imprint of Penguin Random House LLC, 2023

Visit us online at PenguinRandomHouse.com.

Library of Congress Cataloging-in-Publication Data is available.

Printed in the United States of America

ISBN 9780593204412

1st Printing

LSCC

Design by Kate Renner
Text set in New Baskerville ITC

The art for this book was made using graphite and gouache, and then colored digitally.

For Phoebe, and all our giggles

Chapter ONE

Far away from you, there is an ordinary town. In that town, the birds are chirping, the sun is shining, and upon first inspection, nothing would seem out of place. But in this ordinary town, there are peculiar figures and unusual happenings. In hot pursuit of these mysteries are three little girls named Peggy, Rita, and Dot. They, too, seem ordinary upon first inspection. But if you got to know them well and they began to trust you, you might learn something extraordinary: they were young spies in training, studying under the tutelage of

SARAH
AARONSOHN

ODETTE
HALLOWES

JOSEPHINE
BAKER

MARY JANE
RICHARDS DENMAN

CECILY
LEFORT

NOOR INAYAT
KAHN

YOLANDE
BEEKMAN

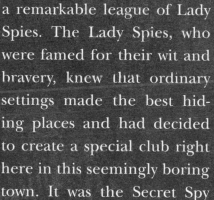

a remarkable league of Lady Spies. The Lady Spies, who were famed for their wit and bravery, knew that ordinary settings made the best hiding places and had decided to create a special club right here in this seemingly boring town. It was the Secret Spy Society.

CHRISTINE
GRANVILLE

NANCY
WAKE

SARAH
EDMONDS

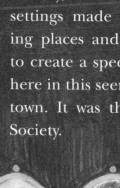

VIRGINIA
HALL

VIOLETTE
SZABO

Peggy, Rita, and Dot aspired to be just like the Lady Spies: assigned to clandestine missions, sent off to mysterious locales, and encouraged to mingle with the brightest and most mysterious figures of their time. But for now, they were known as the Petite Private Eyes.

And today, they were just students. Right now they were—HONK! —at band practice.

The desks shook. **BONK!**
The chalk rattled.
SQUEAK!

In the distance, a stray dog howled along to the bombastic melodies.

Ahh-rooooooo!

It was a typical Tuesday afternoon. The girls had begun learning to play musical instruments this year, and the whole class was working hard to prepare for the spring concert. At the front of the room was the music director, a stern man named Mr. Volrath. The students followed along diligently, keeping one eye on the flick of his baton moving in 4/4 time.

Dot, who had a knack for moving quickly and solving problems with her hands, had naturally gravitated toward the drums. She stood at the back of the band, following Mr. Volrath intently and pattering along to the beat.

Rita, who had an aptitude for all things mathematical and logical, had begun studying the saxophone. All the complex keys and tones fascinated her, and she was quickly becoming an expert at her scales and arpeggios.

Peggy, who was silly and loud and full of tricks, had chosen the *womp*s and *woop*s of the trombone. Peggy saw opportunities for jokes and diversions all around—even in band class.

As the band approached their final notes, a thought crossed Peggy's mind: time for a solo! The song tapered off to a soft diminuendo, but Peggy did the opposite. She crescendoed, growing louder and louder, her trombone slide wiggling back and forth as she made a great, wild, howling—

Giggles broke out all over the room.

Mr. Volrath, however, was not so amused.

"Peggy . . ." he began, sighing deeply. "How many times have I told you that this is *not* the Peggy show?"

Peggy knew she should feel bad, but she just couldn't help herself. *Just one more joke,* she thought. Peggy brought the trombone back to her lips and blew a forlorn:

WOMP WOMP...

"That's it!" Mr. Volrath didn't usually lose his temper, but now his mustache twitched wildly. "This is practice time for the *band*! The *whole* band! One more disruption and you're out of the spring concert!"

Peggy rolled her eyes and her cheeks flushed hot. Her stomach twisted with anger and embarrassment. *Mr. Volrath stinks,* she thought to herself.

The music director composed himself, smoothing his crisp button-down shirt and clearing his throat. "Terrific work today, kids. I can tell you have all been practicing a lot at home. But we have *some* work to do"—he shot a meaningful look at Peggy— "though I am thrilled with our progress.

"As a reminder, our concert is less than a week away." Throughout the room, students groaned. Mr. Volrath raised his hands apologetically. "I know, I know! Sunday is also the math club competition. But we can't change the date now. It's simply too late." He smoothed his mustache thoughtfully. "I know it's difficult, but students who are part of both groups must choose which event they will attend. Class dismissed!"

The students sprang from their seats and the room filled with chatter about homework and recess plans and the upcoming spring concert.

"Tough luck there, Peggy," said Dot with a grimace.

Rita nodded. "Mr. Volrath just wants what's best for the band, but I wish he hadn't scolded you."

Peggy shrugged. "Mr. Volrath just can't take a joke, and it's not my fault that he doesn't like me." She pulled out her trombone case. "On a more important note: Rita, have you decided what you're going to do about the math club competition?"

"You *are* their star member!" said Dot with a grin.

Rita frowned. Math clubbers and band students had been asking her this every day since Mr. Volrath had announced the conflicting dates. "Math club is fine, but I love band! And you guys." She shrugged and began taking apart her saxophone. "It's the obvious choice!"

Just as the girls bent to put their instruments away, a flurry of bouncing curls came dashing toward them.

It was their classmate Ivy. "My oboe!" she cried. She barreled through the room, pushing classmates out of the way as she looked frantically around under chairs and behind bass drums. Reeds flew through the air and tambourines rolled across the floor. "I can't find it!"

She nearly toppled into Rita, who steadied her gently by the shoulders.

"Ivy," she said calmy. "What happened?"

Ivy wiped a tear from her cheek. "I went to the bathroom right after our last song," she sniffled. "When I came back, my oboe was gone!"

Dot and Peggy had gathered around. "Gone?" asked Dot, patting her drumsticks on her leg.

"Gone!" cried Ivy. Peggy, Rita, and Dot nodded at one another. A missing oboe? Local mysteries were their specialty, and they happened to have an opening in their busy schedule.

Dot took Ivy's hand. "The Petite Private Eyes are on the case!"

–*–*–*–

The next day, Hannah was distraught over her missing piccolo and Matthew announced to the group that his tuba had vanished into thin air! Mr. Volrath scratched his head. "How could someone steal a tuba?" he said.

It just didn't seem possible. But somehow the situation grew even more dire as the week progressed. A missing mouthpiece here, a stolen saxophone reed there. By Friday the band room was missing:

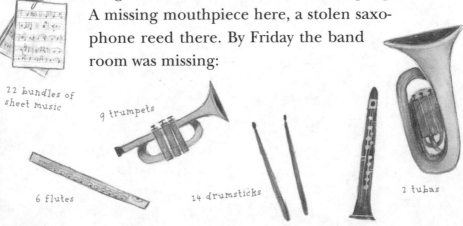

22 bundles of sheet music

9 trumpets

6 flutes

14 drumsticks

2 tubas

8 clarinets

5 trombones

16 reeds

9 mouthpieces

1 sousaphone

And then, seemingly under her nose, Peggy's trombone was gone. "I can't believe it! I put it away here," she cried. Mr. Volrath seemed to squint at her across the room. He shook his head. Peggy's cheeks began to burn. Was he thinking *she* was the instrument thief? Is that why he was shaking his head? This cranky mustachioed man was out to get her no matter what happened!

In band class, Mr. Volrath was grim. Half of the melody was lost and the harmonies were clunky. Some students sat awkwardly twiddling their thumbs, while others tried to whistle their parts (this was complicated by the fact that most students could not actually whistle).

At the end of practice, Mr. Volrath gathered everyone around. With slumped shoulders he addressed the band wearily. "What has happened is devastating. And at this rate, we can no longer function as a band. If we can't find these instruments by our Saturday morning dress rehearsal, I'm afraid we'll need to cancel the spring concert." He shook his head in disbelief.

The room filled with wails of despair, but not from Peggy, Rita, and Dot. Private Eyes do *not* give in easily. Besides, now this was *personal*.

An investigation inside one's school has pros and cons.

PROS:

—Easy to keep your friends close & your enemies closer
—We know all the best hiding spots

CONS:

—HOW DO WE HOLD A PROPER INVESTIGATION WHEN TEACHERS ARE CONSTANTLY LOOKING OVER OUR SHOULDERS???

The girls knew this investigation would prove difficult, but even they couldn't have predicted the challenges. While collecting intel in study hall, they tried to use their flashlights to send messages with Morse code. To their dismay, the substitute teacher caught them mid-signal and confiscated their flashlights. And later, they tried to pass top-secret intel on a paper airplane, but Mr. Volrath intercepted their message and scolded Peggy (again) in front of the whole class.

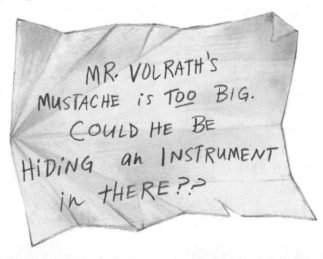

MR. VOLRATH'S MUSTACHE is TOO BIG. COULD HE BE HiDiNG an INSTRUMENT in tHERE??

Now they were defeated, flashlight-less, and stuck nursing their bruised egos in the stinky cafeteria.

"This is completely and utterly embarrassing," grumbled Peggy as she slid onto the bench.

"Maybe we were a *bit* overconfident in our abilities," sighed Dot as she munched on leftovers from home. Rita was eating a crisp tuna sandwich while Peggy investigated a soggy chicken nugget from the cafeteria.

"We need a way to communicate without everyone intercepting our messages," said Rita, taking a thoughtful bite from her pickle.

"Mr. Volrath is the worst," said Peggy, cautiously nibbling. "It's probably his fault. If he would just move the concert, that would give us more time to investigate *and* fix this whole math club debacle!"

Rita groaned. "Everyone in math club keeps pressuring me to skip the band concert! I'm stressed."

Peggy tried to force down one of the repulsive chicken nuggets. "I give up!" She peeled herself from the sticky cafeteria bench to put her lunch tray away.

Dot and Rita gasped. "Peggy!" Dot hissed. "What is that?"

Peggy tilted her tray. To her surprise, she found a small envelope taped to the bottom. In tidy cursive it said TO THE PETITE PRIVATE EYES.

Dear Peggy, Rita, and Dot,
Please join us for tea on Friday. Arrive promptly after the last school bell rings.
XOXO
—N.K.

Tick, tock... tick, tock...

The hands of the clock moved dreadfully slow that afternoon. Peggy, Rita, and Dot could not wait for the day to end. As the last school bell rang, the girls shot out of their seats.

Where were they headed? A mysterious place they had discovered a few months ago: the Secret Spy Society. They traced a now-familiar path through winding cobblestone streets and misty alleyways. Finally, they stopped at a nondescript door on a quiet block. Rita eagerly stepped forward and raised her finger to the bell.

Ding! Dong!

The girls grinned and waited patiently for the usual routine to unfold. First, the door opened a crack. Next, a familiar pair of warm brown eyes peered back at them. Then, closer to the ground, a furry nose poked out. The mysterious figure flung the door open.

It was Josephine Baker and her pet cheetah, Chiquita!

"Welcome, girls!"

Inside, the house was full of fascinating trinkets and curious clues, like blueprints and maps, intricate rugs and comfy chairs, compasses and fountain pens, and bottles of ink. In the kitchen they could see Miss Khan. She was one of Peggy, Rita, and Dot's teachers, and through their own sleuthing they had discovered that she was also a highly trained spy. She was standing in front of the stove as a kettle howled.

Aaaahoooo!

"You're just in time!" She smiled.

By this point, the girls had an unspoken system with the Lady Spies: cocoa first, problem solving second. But today, Miss Khan already had a large tray packed full of mugs and topped with a steaming kettle.

Something was amiss. The house was usually buzzing with activity: women bustling with new intel or seeking help on tricky problems or simply gathering to relax while Josephine played one of her songs on the piano. But today, the house was empty except for Miss Khan and Josephine.

"Where is everyone?" asked Peggy.

Josephine's eyes twinkled slyly. "Follow us."

She waved them toward the back door. Miss Khan followed closely as they exited to the garden. Overgrown flowers leaped wildly over the narrow pathway, and tree branches stretched lazily overhead to create a patchwork roof. At the back of the yard was another building, hidden and forgotten behind a beard of vines. The girls had noticed what appeared to be a garden shed through the kitchen window but never thought twice about it.

Miss Khan approached the wooden door, which was covered in chipping paint and dusty layers of dirt. She turned to the girls. "It is of the utmost importance that what you're about to see stays absolutely secret." The girls nodded solemnly. Miss Khan was very wise, and the girls knew when to listen closely. Seeing that they understood, she removed a small key from her pants pocket. It caught a glimmer from the moon as she gently twisted it into the lock.

CLICK!

Peggy, Rita, and Dot had long since learned to expect the unexpected when it came to the Secret Spy Society. But this?

"Wow," mumbled Rita.

"Holy smokes," muttered Dot.

Peggy, not typically at a loss for words, just stared with her jaw agape.

Where there should have been peeling boards and dusty shelves, there were instead wallpapered walls and tidily tiled floors.

Where there should have been garden tools and boxes of forgotten junk, there were instead many rows of neat desks, smartly outfitted with lamps and pencils.

And behind each desk sat a woman. Some were bent over their workstations writing furiously. Others

sat tilted in their seats, chewing the ends of their pencils and lost in thought. Some were paused to sip coffee and chat, slouched toward one another sharing hushed giggles. At the sound of the door opening, the women looked up from their work, acutely aware of three newcomers. Their faces brightened as they realized these newcomers were children.

Peggy, Rita, and Dot were amazed. The Secret Spy Society was full of surprises, yet this surprised them still.

"Who are these women?" asked Peggy quietly as they walked through the rows of desks.

"My darlings, you are in the presence of the most incredible group of code breakers in the world," Miss Khan whispered with a mischievous grin.

"Codes!" the girls gasped. They paced through the aisles, peeking over shoulders and catching glimpses of complex scribbles between the quick scratching of pencils. They saw detailed handmade charts and stacks of crumbled paper, magnifying classes, calculators, and chalkboards full of indecipherable notes.

"This is perfect timing!" exclaimed Rita. "We need to create a code for a case we're solving! It will allow us to communicate better with one another while we're at school."

Dot nodded seriously. "We could really use their help. We are experts at many things, but we have no idea how to create a code."

"We had a feeling that might be the case," said Josephine, smiling slyly. The Lady Spies had a way of knowing things. Josephine guided them to the back of the cavernous room where a woman sat hunched over a large sheet of paper. She sipped tea while studying the symbols before her. She peeled her eyes away from the paper as the girls approached.

"Meet Elizebeth," said Miss Khan.

The woman behind the desk paused from her work and peered up at them from under the brim of her hat. She had a sparkle in her eye. She stood up, extending a hand.

"What a pleasure to meet our three bright young spies!" she said warmly, giving them each a firm handshake. "I've heard wonderful things about you." Her face opened into a wide smile.

Peggy leaned in closer. "You look familiar," she said suspiciously, eyeing Elizebeth up and down.

The woman let out a big laugh. "You're right! You might know me as Mrs. Friedman. I used to be the principal at your school!"

The girls looked back and forth between Miss Khan and Elizebeth in shock.

"Miss Khan is a teacher there!" exclaimed Rita.

Elizebeth chuckled. "Believe it or not, many of the women here are teachers! Others are musicians, some are librarians, others are office workers, but all of us have been trained to make and break top-secret codes!"

Miss Khan nodded. "These women have background training that makes them excellent code makers and brilliant code breakers! We're hosting them here at the Secret Spy Society while they await their next posting. But they're still on the job, which is why it's imperative that you keep this whole affair top secret."

The girls nodded, now understanding Miss Khan's seriousness.

The girls assembled themselves around a spare desk while Elizebeth swept aside eraser shavings and crumbled balls of paper.

"One way to begin is to ask yourself why you need a code in the first place." She pulled out a fresh sheet of paper. "Where will it be used? Why does it need to be secret?"

The girls thought for a moment. "Well, we're trying to solve our case while we're in school, and we need to keep teachers and classmates from seeing what we write," Peggy began.

Elizebeth nodded. "And how should the code be used? Some codes are written, others are sung into the

air. In fact, some are even drawn onto yarn and then knit into a sweater!" The girls giggled.

"It should probably be written," ventured Rita. "We can't exactly be singing to each other in class or knitting sweaters on the school bus!"

"The first rule of being a cryptographer is to work as a team. Always remember that." Elizebeth looked at them seriously, then pulled out a sheet of paper. "Now, let's talk about ciphers. When creating a cipher, we replace each letter of the alphabet with a different letter or symbol. Some ciphers, like the ones we solve, are dizzyingly complex. Some ciphers have been so confusing that even the people who created them can't figure them out!" The girls giggled, imagining words and letters getting jumbled and melted together like marshmallows in hot cocoa.

"Our code should probably be complex enough to stop nosy teachers from reading over our shoulders, but simple enough that we can decode them between classes," said Rita, grinning excitedly. "What if we used symbols?"

PETITE PRIVATE EYE
≡ SUPER-SECRET CIPHER ≡

A: ♭

B: △

C: ♡

D: △

E: ∧

F: ✳

G: ♡

H: ⁒

I: ⋒

J: ✕

K: ⸮

L: ⅃

M: ⌂

N: φ

O: ⊏

P: ⬤

Q: ⊐

R: ⭘

S: ✮

T: □

U: ⊕

V: ⧖

W: ⌒

X: ⊶

Y: ○

Z: ▽

Elizabeth clapped. "Now we're talking!" She slid the paper and three pencils over to the girls.

"This is the coolest code ever!" cheered Dot.

Elizabeth beamed. "Fabulous!" she said as she looked over the symbols. "And now, let's talk about codes. At first glance, codes and ciphers seem the same. But codes replace entire words, phrases, or names with a symbol or another word. For example—"

She pointed her pencil sneakily to Miss Khan, who was sitting on the other side of the room sipping tea and chatting with a group of spies.

"—Miss Khan could have a code name. Like . . . Pookie or Lemon Drop! Or her real code name, which is Madeleine."

The girls giggled.

"To finish off your Petite Private Eye language, you each need a code name or symbol!"

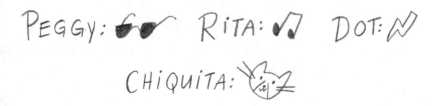

"Let's practice!" said Rita, ever the planner.

"I'll leave you to it!" said Elizebeth, returning to her desk.

"I have an idea," said Peggy. She took a fresh sheet of paper and began furiously scribbling, unable to contain her giggles about what she was writing. Dot tried to peek, but Peggy shooed her away.

"Okay, here you go!" She slid the message across the table.

Rita and Dot got to work decoding. *Chiquita smells like . . .*

They burst out laughing. "She *does* smell like tuna sandwiches!" Chiquita wasn't so amused.

"Can I go next, please? I have an idea!" said Rita, already giggling. She started furiously copying symbols from the master code sheet.

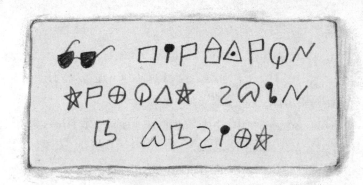

Peggy and Dot began decoding bit by bit. *Peggy's trombone sounds like . . .*

Dot burst out in giggles. "It *does* occasionally sound like a walrus!"

Peggy didn't think that was quite so funny. Her stomach sank. "A walrus?" she asked, mustering a laugh. "Ouch."

"So what's our plan for tomorrow?" asked Rita, always keeping the girls on track. "It's our last chance to save the band concert!"

"Well, we should all have a copy of the cipher," said Dot. "I'll handle that!" Dot liked to work with her hands while she was thinking and began to copy out the Super-Secret Petite Private Eye Cipher for Peggy and Rita.

Rita nodded. "And we should probably sort through any clues we have. We still have no idea who could be behind the missing instruments."

Dot looked up from her flurry of writing to nod. "Yeah! I heard someone in science class saying they were missing their saxophone mouthpiece. And in art class, someone said their trumpet was gone! That indicates *many* possible suspects."

Peggy scoffed. "The culprit is so obvious!" Rita and Dot looked confused. "It's Mr. Volrath!"

Rita and Dot exchanged a glance. "Why, Peggy?" asked Rita.

"*Pffffft!*" Peggy blew a raspberry. "He ruined our investigation today, plus he picks on me *all* the time in class!"

Now Dot spoke up. "But Peggy . . . maybe he's upset because you always joke around."

Rita nodded. "I *love* your jokes!" she said. "But sometimes you interrupt what Mr. Volrath is saying."

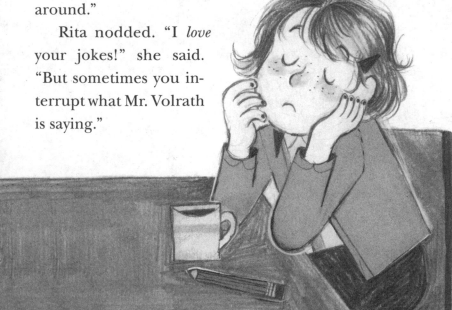

Now Miss Khan and Elizebeth looked up from their work. "Mr. Volrath?" said Miss Khan quizzically. "I've never seen him act suspicious."

Peggy looked annoyed. "The answer is right in front of us. We just need to find the proof."

Dot laughed. "But why would our *band* teacher ruin his own concert? That doesn't make *any* sense!"

"Besides, you can't go searching for evidence to *prove* a theory you already have." Rita shook her head. "That's bad investigating!"

Now Peggy stood up. "Why can't you just take my side?"

Dot and Rita were startled. "We didn't mean to upset—"

But Peggy was already packing her bags. "If you don't believe me, I'll just prove it myself!" She huffed, snatching her copy of the code. "Let's go, Chiquita! We don't need their help."

Dot and Rita sat frozen at the table. "Peggy, wait!" they called. But it was too late. Peggy was out the door.

"What was that about?" asked Elizebeth. She peered up from her work, clearly confused.

"Peggy was upset that we didn't believe her," Rita cried. "We still need more evidence to solve our case, but she wouldn't listen."

Elizebeth thought for a moment. "It sounds like she needs some time alone, girls," she said softly. "Best to give her some space."

"Why won't they believe me?"

Peggy was walking down the street as fast as her legs would carry her. Her shoes made an angry

TAP TAP TAP

as she rounded the corner. Chiquita followed close behind.

"It's so obvious that Mr. Volrath has it out for me."

Chiquita blinked back.

"If we're really a team, shouldn't they take my side?" Chiquita didn't have a response.

A soft rain began to fall and the sky grew darker. Peggy felt even more defeated.

Up ahead, the lights of the school glowed through the dusky air. "You have to wait out here, Chiquita. I can't bring a cheetah into school, even after hours!" Chiquita looked sad, but Peggy patted her on the head. "I'll be right back."

She brushed the raindrops off her jacket, tightened up her backpack straps, and pulled open the front doors.

Chapter TWO

Back at the Secret Spy Society, Elizebeth and Miss Khan joined Rita and Dot at their table.

"The spring concert is only two days away. We need to try to solve the case or it will be canceled," Dot said.

Rita turned to a new page in her notebook. A crisp, white page always helped her think clearly. "So," she said, sharpening her pencil. "What next?"

"Let's consider the motive," said Miss
Khan. "Why might someone want to
steal instruments?"

"Maybe they want to be a rock
star?" Dot giggled.

"Maybe they collect shiny
things?" chortled Rita. The girls
managed a laugh but then fell into
a silence.

"I wish Peggy were
here," said Dot glumly.
"She's good at thinking
outside of the box."

−*−*−*−

WOOOSH! went the door.

The school was silent except for the *squick squick* of Peggy's shoes on the freshly mopped floors.

"I'll prove that I don't need anyone's help!" Peggy mumbled to herself. She hurried past empty classrooms, where a handful of teachers were still packing up their things or preparing lessons.

Left, right, down the stairs. The silence that hung over the school made her shiver.

"Come on, Peggy," she whispered to herself. "You've solved mysteries way scarier than this!" She moved quicker and quicker, palms sweating the closer she got to the band room. As much as she wanted to be calm, Peggy really was nervous. Mr. Volrath had seemed so angry in class. What would he do if he found her snooping around after hours?

She peeked through the window in the band room door. Inside, instruments and cases were tucked into cubbies and sheet music littered the floor. *The perfect place to find evidence*, she thought to herself.

Peggy unzipped her backpack and began looking for something to pick the lock with. Dot was an expert lock picker. What was that tool she always used?

"Rats," she muttered under her breath. "Rita would have packed a screwdriver or a paper clip. No matter!" She unfastened a barrette from her hair. "If Dot can do it, so can I!" But when Peggy tried to pick the lock, nothing happened. *Dot makes this look so easy*, she thought to herself, hands getting sweatier as she fumbled with the lock.

"Hello, Peggy," said a voice from down the hall.

EEEP! squeaked Peggy. The barrette flew into the air.

—*—*—*—*—

"I have an idea!" said Rita. "Why don't we look through the yearbook? The culprit must be in there somewhere, and this might help us to consider all the suspects." She pulled it out of her backpack.

Dot's jaw dropped. "How are you always so prepared, Rita?"

Rita shrugged. "We're solving a mystery about our *school*! It's only natural to keep a yearbook on hand." She cracked open the spine and flipped through.

"Hmmmm . . . what about him?" Dot pointed to a photo of a student with glasses and a

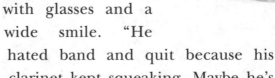

wide smile. "He hated band and quit because his clarinet kept squeaking. Maybe he's jealous that everyone else is having fun?"

Rita shrugged. "But he really likes ballet. I think he's having too much fun with pliés and grand jetés to be jealous." She scanned the next page, pointing to a girl with a head of neat braids. "Well, what about her?"

"Maybe," said Dot. "She was disappointed Mr. Volrath chose Beethoven over Copland for the concert. But she loves the violin. She wouldn't want to miss out on playing it."

Rita shook her head. "This is pointless, Dot! We don't have evidence or any motives."

"You're right," grumbled Dot. She flipped lazily through the pages until something caught her eye on the extracurricular activities page. "Hold on!" she said.

Both girls leaned in close for a better look.

–*–*–*–

"Matthew!" Peggy sighed with relief. "You startled me!"

She stood up to face her classmate: class president, valedictorian, soccer captain, tuba player, and head of the math club. He smiled sweetly and bent to pick up Peggy's fallen barrette.

"I'm here studying for math club all weekend. But what are you doing here, Peggy?" asked

Matthew. "You look a little . . . lost." He glanced around at the empty hallway.

Peggy mustered a smile. "I'm just doing some . . . extra studying. But I'm a little . . . stuck."

Matthew nodded. "I understand that feeling. Why don't we talk about it in the math club room?"

Peggy knew she should focus on her case, but the band door was locked anyway, and she knew for a fact that the math club kept a well-stocked bowl of candy in their meeting room. She could practically *taste* the chocolates in her mouth. What was the harm?

Reese

Daisy

Sara

Andrea

John

Tamar

MATTHEW
President of the Math Club,
reigning champions

–*–*–*–

"How could it *possibly* be him?" asked Rita. "He's the best student in our class!"

"Besides *you*, obviously," said Dot, elbowing Rita with a laugh. Then she was serious. "He's been so frustrated that the band concert is the same night as the math club competition."

Rita nodded. "He was so upset when I told him I would go to the band concert instead."

Elizebeth gazed down at the book. "Remember, as spies, it's your job to gather information, *not* to jump to conclusions."

"But it's good to listen to your instincts," Miss Khan added. "He *is* quite an ambitious student. That's usually a good thing . . . except when it goes too far. Perhaps you can look into it tomorrow at school."

Rita and Dot nodded.

"Tomorrow."

– * – * – * –

Inside the math club room, desks were arranged into neat parallelograms. The room was small but tidily packed with all sorts of equipment. Calculus books filled the shelves—spines perfectly aligned—and pens and highlighters sat in jars, organized by color and size. The chalkboard was covered in complex algebra and lengthy trigonometry solutions (admittedly, Peggy didn't understand the numbers).

Matthew held out the candy bowl. "So," he began. "What's got you stuck?"

Peggy concentrated on unwrapping her chocolate. Truthfully, she was unsure whether or not she should tell Matthew about their mission. On one hand, this was top secret and she only shared intel with Rita and Dot. But on the other hand, Matthew was at the top of their class. He might know something useful. *Besides,* she thought to herself, *Rita and Dot aren't here!*

"Actually," she began, popping the chocolate into her mouth. "I'm trying to solve a mystery."

"A mystery?" asked Matthew. He seemed amused.

"Yes," Peggy continued cautiously. "You know how the musical instruments have been disappearing, like your tuba?"

"Yes." Matthew raised an eyebrow.

Peggy nodded solemnly. "I'm convinced that Mr. Volrath is behind it. He's had it out for me all year."

Matthew nodded. "He has no sense of humor."

"That's what I always say!" Peggy exclaimed. "Our spring concert is on Sunday, and it's going to be canceled if we don't get our instruments back. It's a really big . . ." Something behind Matthew caught her eye. ". . . problem."

Behind Matthew, a storage cabinet had creaked open. Peggy noticed something protruding out.

Was that her trombone case, along with a bunch of instruments?

Peggy looked at the cabinet, then looked at Matthew.

Matthew looked at the cabinet, then back at Peggy.

Peggy's stomach suddenly felt sour and sticky, the way it felt when she ate too many chocolates. She fiddled with her barrette and cleared her throat, trying not to let her nervousness show.

Matthew's demeanor changed. In one moment, he
had gone from friendly to cold as ice. His expression
fell and he quickly pulled back the dish of chocolates.
Matthew stood up. "Time for me to study."
Before Peggy could react, Matthew moved quickly
through the desks. He grabbed some of the instrument

cases and was and out the door, swiftly locking it behind him.

Peggy was trapped.

"But why?" Peggy cried.

Matthew's face twisted with frustration. "Isn't it obvious? The math club *needs* Rita in order to win. She's the secret to our success, and without her we don't stand a chance. No band concert means no chance of losing Rita." He smoothed his tie. "Now if you'll excuse me, I need to start moving some of these instruments to a new hiding spot. I'll be back for more soon, and then you can go."

"The show will go on somehow!" she cried. "I'll tell Mr. Volrath what you did!"

"Would Mr. Volrath believe *you*, the class clown? Or me, the best student in our class?" Matthew's face split into a devious grin. "Besides, it doesn't matter. The band will never find the instruments in time. And I'll return them on Monday."

–*–*–*–

Back at the Secret Spy Society, Rita and Dot were ready to call it quits. "I'm getting tired, and I still have so much homework to do," sighed Dot.

Rita closed a copy of *All About Codes*. "I agree. Let's resume tomorrow."

Elizebeth, still working diligently nearby, stood up to walk them to the door.

"Good work today, girls. If there's anything I've learned from my time as a cryptographer, it's patience. You can't have a breakthrough every day!"

"That's true," said Rita, rubbing her bleary eyes. "But I thought Peggy would have come back by now?"

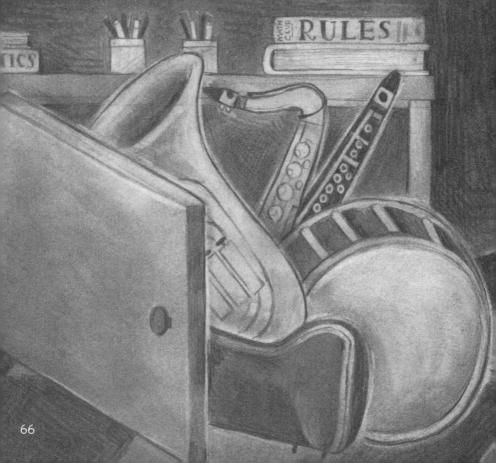

"Think, Peggy, think!" she whispered to herself. "What would Dot and Rita do? What would the Lady Spies do?" She began to cry softly. Dot and Rita would've never let this happen in the first place! Everything would be better if they were here.

Through her tears, she heard a soft *skritch skritch* on the window. Peggy looked out. Chiquita!

Peggy tried to pry the window open but it would only budge an inch. She reached her finger out to scratch Chiquita's soft furry nose. "I'm so glad you're here!" she whispered to the cheetah, wiping a tear from her cheek.

Think, Peggy.

"Aha!"

She rifled through the room until she found a scrap of paper. Then she pulled out a note from her pocket. The Super-Secret Petite Private Eye Cipher! She wrote furiously.

Gently, she folded the paper and slipped it through the window to Chiquita. "Take this to the Secret Spy Society," she whispered. "They'll know what to do!"

Chiquita understood. She sped off into the night.

Chapter
THREE

Rita and Dot zipped their backpacks. "Are you sure Peggy is okay?" asked Dot.

Elizebeth put a hand gently on her shoulder. "She was quite upset earlier. Perhaps she went back home and decided to call it a night?"

In the midst of gathering their notebooks and saying goodbye, they noticed a soft *skritch skritch* at the door. It was quiet at first, not much louder than the wind, but grew more and more persistent until the door was nearly shaking. Elizebeth approached cautiously, opening it a crack.

In flew a flurry of spots. Chiquita! She shook her fluffy coat, flinging droplets of rain all over. Dot began drying off the damp cheetah when something occurred to her. "Wait a moment," she said. "If you're back . . . Where's Peggy?"

"Look, Dot!" gasped Rita. "What's that in her mouth?"

Rita and Dot returned to the table, pulling out their cipher and translating the message as quickly as they could.

The girls gasped and stared wildly at one another. "We were right!" Then Rita's face turned to horror. "But if she's sending this note . . . she must be stuck!"

Dot put on her helmet. "Let's go!"

The spies wasted no time. Quick as lightning but quiet as a breeze, they shut their notebooks and put their tea aside. The cryptographers weren't specifically trained in undercover operations, but they followed behind silently.

Chiquita led the way, carefully tracing the path back. Miss Khan, still equipped with her keys to the school, carefully opened the front doors. Even in the after-hours silence, the Lady Spies managed to walk without making a single sound on the hard tile floors.

"This way!" whispered Dot, pointing in the direction of the math club meeting room.

"Look!" whispered Dot.

There was Peggy! Her nose was pressed to the glass door of the math club room as she called out to them. In the darkness, the books behind her looked like teeth, ready to chomp down any moment. Her face suddenly filled with horror.

"What's she trying to say?" asked Rita. Peggy's face grew more and more panicked.

"Why is she pointing to us?" wondered Dot. "Unless . . ."

Peggy and Rita turned around slowly. Looming behind them was Matthew.

"Hello, girls." Matthew grinned. "What a coinci-
dence seeing you here."

"Let Peggy go!" yelled Dot.

"No, thanks. I'd prefer that you join her, actually,
while I finish out my plan." He took a step forward.

Miss Khan and Elizebeth emerged from the shadows. Matthew's face went pale with surprise at the sight of his teacher and former principal standing in front of him.

"Miss Khan! Mrs. Friedman!" he stammered, tightening his tie. "What are you doing here so late?"

They crossed their arms. "It sounds like you have some explaining to do."

The Petite Private Eyes knew just what to do next.

Rita quickly unzipped her backpack, knowing exactly where to find the screwdriver. She passed it to Dot, who got to work on the door. In mere seconds the lock popped open and the girls rushed inside.

"I'm so sorry!" cried Peggy, hugging her friends tightly. "I got angry and thought I could do everything myself!"

Rita squeezed her hand. "It's okay. Even when we disagree, we don't need to fight."

Dot nodded. "Who's right and who's wrong isn't important. But how we make each other feel *is* important!"

Peggy wiped a tear from her cheek. "Thank you for finding me," she said softly. "Friends forever?"

"Friends forever!"

–*–*–*–

Peggy, Rita, and Dot emerged from the math club room
carrying as many instruments as their arms could hold.
The Lady Spies grinned. "Need a hand?"

One by one, hushed as only spies can be, they carried the musical instruments back to the band room. And as silently as they had entered the school, they swiftly exited and disappeared into the night on their way to some well-earned rest.

BUUURRR...

hummed the warmup note.

The night had finally arrived. Each student put on their best outfit, buckled their shoes, polished their brass, and filed into the band room for their very first spring concert. They were one tuba player short, since Matthew had been suspended from school after being caught with the missing instruments, but the rest of the band would play on!

Rita adjusted Peggy's barrettes while Dot folded her bowtie.

"What if I make a mistake?" whispered Rita nervously as she put together her saxophone.

Peggy grinned. "Then your friends will be right alongside you to help."

Mr. Volrath led the band in single file to the stage, where each student stood in front of their designated chairs.

"You've all worked so hard and will shine like stars tonight," he said, smoothing his mustache. "I am proud of each and every one of you!" He caught Peggy's eye and gave a wink.

The curtain opened with a

Swooosh!

And through the bright lights they could make out a large group filing in and taking seats at the front of the auditorium.

The Lady Spies! Peggy and Rita fought back wide grins as they raised their instruments to their lips. Dot resisted the urge to wave her drumsticks from the back of the stage.

Mr. Volrath raised his baton and began to count off.

Butterflies danced and twirled in the girl's stomachs, but they knew they could handle a concert, even if every note wasn't perfect. They had each other. And after all, what's a little stage fright to three world-class Petite Private Eyes?

The crowd began to applaud.

ABOUT CIPHERS AND CODES

The art of making and breaking ciphers and codes—also called cryptology—has long been an important tool for spies. There's a difference between ciphers and codes: ciphers replace letters of the alphabet with other letters or symbols in order to scramble a message. Codes replace entire words. A good cipher is one that is easy for your allies to read, but complicated enough to keep your message safe from prying eyes. Codebreaking is an equally useful skill: if a spy is able to break into her enemy's codes, she has access to all of their secrets.

Some ciphers, like the Petite Private Eyes' Super-Secret Cipher, are easy to read if there's a key to explain the symbols, also called a "code book." But others, like ones used by Germany and Japan during World War II, are very complex and contain layers and layers of confusing encryption. A code like that can only be cracked though devoted teamwork.

To break ciphers, cryptanalysts search for coincidences, patterns, and repetitions. Certain letters of the English alphabet (like "e" and "r") occur more often than others (like "x" or "z"). Other letters are frequently used in combination (like "th" or "ing") or appear more often at the beginning or ends of words. Using this knowledge, cryptanalysts begin to understand their enemy's cipher.

During World War II, the United States government recruited a special group for the top-secret job of codebreaking: young women. Mysterious letters appeared for them in the mail, summoning them to covert meetings in strange locations where they were asked to take an oath of secrecy. Many of these women were unmarried schoolteachers who were knowledgeable in Latin and literature, which gave them the advantage of understanding language. Others were musicians who had a talent for spotting patterns in coded messages. Some were librarians and secretaries who were skilled at the organization and machine operation necessary for the massive team effort. For

PEGGY: 🐛🐛   RITA: ✓✓   DOT: 🖊

CHIQUITA: 🐱🦴

many of these women, the recruitment was life changing and gave them a freedom that was unusual at the time. African American women were also recruited for cryptanalysis teams, but their teams were segregated due to Jim Crow–era laws. Sadly, many of their identities are still a mystery to this day.

Many female codebreakers at this time were based outside of Washington, DC, in a converted girls' school, and later moved to Sugar Camp in Dayton, Ohio. Sugar Camp looked like any other summer camp, complete with cabins, bunk beds, and lakes for swimming. But, as with most things in espionage, there was more to the camp than met the eye. The cabins were retrofitted with desks and machinery, and the occupants were codebreaking experts. There, the women pored over coded messages and formed lifelong friendships.

One of these talented codebreaking women was Elizebeth Friedman. Elizebeth's interest in codebreaking came from her background in literature, and she was briefly a school principal. In college, she had a particular love for Shakespeare, which led to her unexpected work in cryptography. A wealthy and eccentric merchant hired Elizebeth to search for secret ciphers in Shakespeare's work, which he believed would unveil an alternative identity of the author. Though that task was ultimately a dead end, Elizebeth discovered her love for cryptography.

Elizebeth met her husband, William, while working together on the secretive Shakespeare project, and they had a true marriage of equals. Unfortunately, Elizebeth's work was overshadowed by her husband's, despite the fact that she was the one who had introduced him to cryptography. She worked with the Coast Guard cryptanalysis team during World War II, intercepting messages from a secretive Nazi spy network in South America and leading a team of men, though her achievements were often incorrectly attributed to other people. Today, Elizebeth is remembered as America's first female cryptanalyst and is celebrated for her contribution to the field.

ABOUT THE OTHER LADY SPIES

SARAH AARONSOHN (1890–1917)
Syria. Founded and led an underground network of Jewish spies during World War I.

JOSEPHINE BAKER (1906–1975)
United States. Baker worked as a successful dancer, singer, and actress in France, where she was recruited to aid the French Resistance during World War II. A civil rights activist and entertainment icon, she also had a pet cheetah named Chiquita.

YOLANDE BEEKMAN (1911–1944)

Great Britain. Spoke several languages, which made her especially useful for secretive communications for the Special Operations Executive during World War II.

MARY JANE RICHARDS DENMAN (C. 1840-UNKNOWN)

United States. Also known as Mary Bowser, Denman was a formerly enslaved woman who went undercover in the Confederate South to fight against slavery as a Union Army spy.

SARAH EMMA EDMONDS (1841–1898)

Canada. Disguised herself as a man to help fight against slavery in the Civil War and work as a spy for the Union Army.

CHRISTINE GRANVILLE (1908-1952)

Poland. Also known as Krystyna Skarbek, she was known for her glamour, her style, and her ability to charm everyone (even guard dogs), as she worked for the Special Operations Executive during World War II.

VIRGINIA HALL (1906-1982)

United States. Worked for the American Office of Strategic Services and the CIA after World War II, along with other organizations. She lost one of her legs in a hunting accident, but her prosthetic leg (named Cuthbert) made her excellent at undercover missions.

ODETTE HALLOWES (1912-1995)

Great Britain. Proved herself invaluable to her team at the Special Operations Executive despite her nervous demeanor. Also a mother of three girls, she survived the Ravensbrück concentration camp.

NOOR INAYAT KHAN (1914-1944)

Great Britain. An author of stories and poems for young children, Khan worked as a wireless operator for the Special Operations Executive during World War II. Tragically, she was captured and sent to the Dachau concentration camp. She refused to give up any secrets to her captors, and her final word was rumored to be "liberty."

CECILY LEFORT (1900-1945)

Great Britain. Served in the Women's Auxiliary Air Force and for the Special Operations Executive during World War II. She had excellent manners and liked sailing boats and riding horses.

VIOLETTE SZABO (1921-1945)

France. Worked for the Special Operations Executive during World War II and was highly trained in many specialties, like navigation, demolition, and parachuting. (She could also tell very good jokes.)

NANCY WAKE (1912-2011)

New Zealand. Celebrated for her skills in combat and infamous for her sassy wit, she joined the French Resistance and the Special Operations Executive in World War II.